Copyright © 2020 by Shanta Lamarr

All rights reserved. No part of this book may be reproduced in any form on by an electronic or mechanical means, including information storage and retrieval systems, without permission in writing from the publisher, except by a reviewer who may quote brief passages in a review.

As a child, I grew up In the kitchen along with my maternal grandmother who was my first and greatest Chef. She would make a lot of delicious homemade soups and stews. I have always enjoyed smelling and tasting a lot of flavors. It became a hearty bite. I saw a lot of my family members suffer from food related illnesses, as-well-as myself. I struggled with gastric problems from birth. In my mid- 20's, I started the journey of learning how to be creative with healthier meals. I grew up eating great tasting food, but I learned that food just like love is reciprocated based on Quality. My mission became to ensure that my food was healthy and did not lack flavor.

It's been twelve years of study and preparation....Along my journey, as I began to become more educated concerning: (1) Spirituality, (2) African-American history, and (3) foods, I have discovered that these three are connected in many ways. Over the years, I have tried different styles of eating, while practicing on eliminating food that were conducive to me becoming healthier. The more I reduced the better I felt. I've spent years in pain, trying to be a slave to the ideas that I had to have certain food to feel accepted and complete. I became aware and was awaken to that which I felt nothing could taste as good; I was wrong. The reality is that SOME foods have flavors you cannot replicate without meat. I will say that, collectively with the knowledge which I have gained through my journey long with the flavor that African Americans bring to our soulful cooking, this plant-based diet is just "Better Things To Eat." I became devoted to continue to gain knowledge of food so that I may use Quality foods a long with my inspiration to eat better. This series is the first on Soups and Stews. Its aim is to help people add healthier plant-based dishes that can either replace their normal meals or eat a long with their meals.

The purpose of this to invite you to explore more options and not to convert you to become a vegan. It's a food journey to assist and to educate the audience on the benefits of eating healthier foods. We together, will be introducing new options to your palette. This book is a documented journey of recipes that I have used from Yummly (download the app), I am not a chef, I am giving flowers to all the chefs and food bloggers that have helped me along the way, while showcasing great recipes that I used along with a little twist I added to customize them to my palate. As well as, giving knowledgeable information I learned about food along my journey, these recipes are a lot of foods you already love mixed with some alkaline foods that are essential for your body, take these foods and add some creativity, you have…

BETTER THINGS TO EAT

Series I
Soups and Stews

By Shanta Lamarr

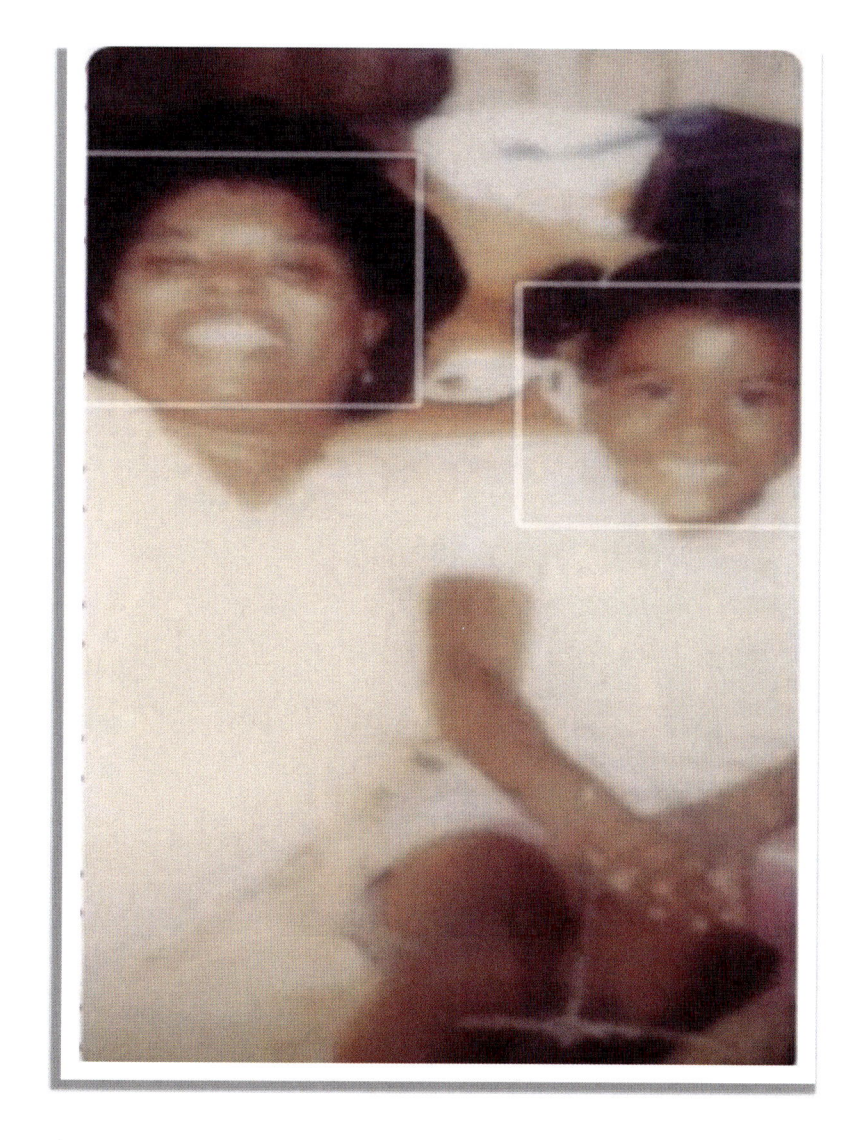

This book is dedicated to my grandmother, the late Mayrose M. Moon who was my first chef. She taught me through love that food is just not used for nourishment of the body, but it's also for love of self as-well-as the soul.

Special thanks to my great-grandmother the late Carrie Lamarr Webb Waugh and my Aunt Vernell Murray-Mason who named me Shanta. The silverware displayed on the cover is gifted from the family collection and the Chinaware is gifted from Aunt Vernell.

Rest in eternal peace, I love You Forever

Table of Contents

Vegan Chickpea Soup - 7

Mulligatawny Soup - 10

Roasted Tomato Pepper Bisque - 13

Black Bean Soup - 15

Vegetable Broth - 19

Caribbean Black-Eyed Peas Stew - 23

Vegan Jackfruit Stew - 25

Creamy Vegan Broccoli Cauliflower Soup - 28

Smoky Vegan Quinoa Chili - 31

Cabbage Soup - 33

Potato Corn Chowder – 35

Suggested Shopping List – 38

14 Day Plant Based Meal Planner - 39

Vegan Chickpea Noodle Soup

Serve- 8

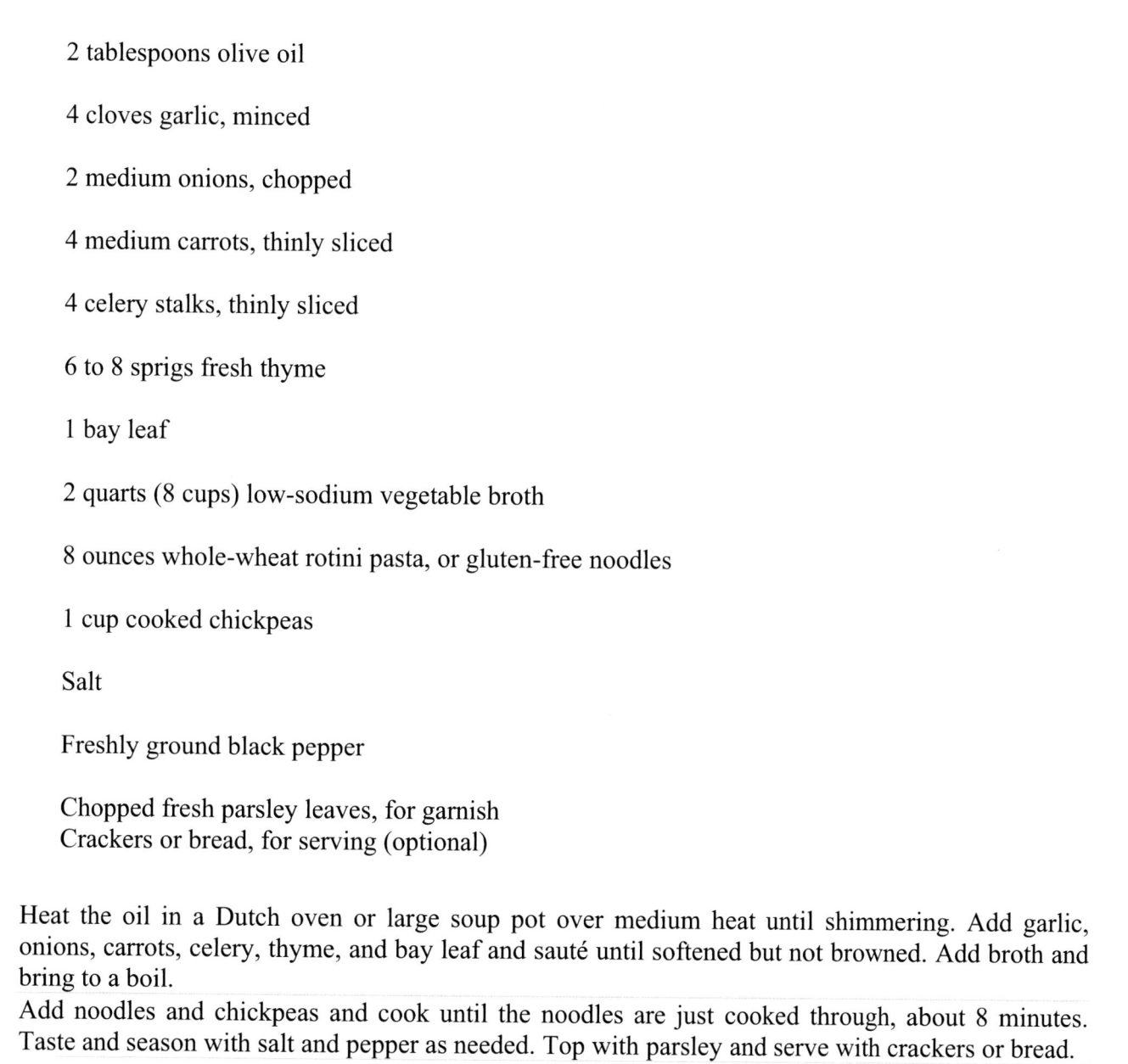

2 tablespoons olive oil

4 cloves garlic, minced

2 medium onions, chopped

4 medium carrots, thinly sliced

4 celery stalks, thinly sliced

6 to 8 sprigs fresh thyme

1 bay leaf

2 quarts (8 cups) low-sodium vegetable broth

8 ounces whole-wheat rotini pasta, or gluten-free noodles

1 cup cooked chickpeas

Salt

Freshly ground black pepper

Chopped fresh parsley leaves, for garnish
Crackers or bread, for serving (optional)

Heat the oil in a Dutch oven or large soup pot over medium heat until shimmering. Add garlic, onions, carrots, celery, thyme, and bay leaf and sauté until softened but not browned. Add broth and bring to a boil.
Add noodles and chickpeas and cook until the noodles are just cooked through, about 8 minutes. Taste and season with salt and pepper as needed. Top with parsley and serve with crackers or bread.

Chickpeas also known as garbanzo bean was something that had to grow on me but after I started playing around with them and trying new recipes, I fell in love.

Chickpeas nutritional benefits are:

- Helps regulate blood sugar
- High in fiber
- Good for weight loss
- Heart Health
- Great source of Protein
- Rich in iron and Vitamin B
- Low sodium helps low blood pressure
- Helps fight inflammation
- Good for eyes, skin and hair
- Balance hormones

Photo Credit & Food: Shanta Lamarr

Mulligatawny Soup

Serve- 8

2 tsp oil
1 cup uncooked red lentils rinsed and cleaned
1 large yellow onion chopped
1 large carrot peeled and diced
3 cloves garlic minced
2 tsp fresh ginger peeled and minced
1 sweet potato, diced
1 14.5 oz can diced tomatoes
1 Tbl curry powder (or paste)
1/2 tsp ground coriander
1/2 tsp ground cinnamon
1/2 tsp ground turmeric
1/4 tsp ground cardamom
1/4 tsp freshly ground black pepper
4 cups low sodium vegetable broth (or 4 cups homemade)
2/3 cup light canned coconut milk (or use 2/3 cup nondairy milk mixed with about 1 tsp coconut extract)
sea salt and pepper to taste
1/3 cup cilantro chopped, and/or scallions for garnish

Add oil to a large pan with the onion, Cook for 5 minutes, stirring regularly, until it starts to brown.

Add carrots, garlic, ginger, sweet potato, and diced tomatoes to the pot. Sauté for another 3 minutes, then add all of the spices and toss to coat.

Add lentil and broth and let the contents come to a boil. Turn the heat down to medium-low and simmer uncovered for 30 minutes. Add more water or broth if it gets too thick.

Transfer about half of the soup, slightly cooled, into a blender and blend until smooth. Then pour back into the pot and stir well. Or use an blender to cream part of the soup in the pot.

Stir in the coconut milk and cook a few more minutes.

Taste, and adjust salt and black pepper as needed.

Serve topped with scallions along with crusty bread or naan for dipping.

Authors Note:

Now this soup right here is like Mack 10, FLAVA in your ears good, it is SOOO good and really good for you! African Americans are 60% more likely to be diagnosed with diabetes than non-Hispanic white adults. Lentils, are high fiber foods which are an important component of a diabetic diet because of their low glycemic index. My grandmother, grandfather and aunt Vernell, as-well-as, other family members suffered from diabetes, this is something, I often worry about for myself so learning that legumes are a great source of nutrient and helps stabilize blood sugar levels was really a gem for me. Other great benefits of lentils:

Brown, green, yellow, red or black lentils

- low in calories,
- rich in iron and folate
- excellent source of protein
- They pack health-promoting polyphenols
- may reduce several heart disease risk factors

Photo Credit & Food: Shanta Lamarr

Roasted Tomato Pepper Bisque

Serving Size – 5

5 large tomatoes quartered
1 medium red bell pepper seeded and quartered
2 large yellow onions quartered
4 cloves garlic peeled
2 1/2 cups low sodium vegetable broth or homemade broth, or water
1/2 cup coconut milk
1/2 tsp paprika
sea salt and pepper to taste

Preheat oven to 400 degrees F. Line a large baking sheet with parchment paper and spread the tomatoes, onions and peppers onto it. Sprinkle with salt, pepper and paprika.

Bake in the oven for about 5 minutes and then add the garlic cloves. Continue to roast the vegetables until they soften and start to caramelize, about 15 minutes, stirring about halfway through. Check to see if they're browning.

Put the vegetables into a large soup pot and add the vegetable broth. Use an immersion blender to process until smooth and then heat through. Or if you'd like to use a blender, add the tomatoes to it after roasting with enough broth to blend. Then add the blended tomatoes to the pot with the rest of the broth and heat through.

Add 1/2 cup of coconut milk stir to combine. Taste and add up to 1/2 cup more, if needed. Season with salt, pepper, and more paprika.

Authors Note:

I have always loved tomato soup, this is something you can easily pair with a grilled cheese, sandwich and/or salad. Great nutritional benefits of Tomatoes

- reduce the risk of heart disease and cancer.
- great source of vitamin C
- potassium
- folate
- and vitamin K

Photo Credit & Food: Shanta Lamarr

Black Bean Soup

Serving- 6

3-4 cups low sodium vegetable broth or water for sauteing.
2-15 oz. cans low sodium black beans rinsed and drained (or 3 cups homemade)
1 large onion diced
1 large sweet potato peeled and cubed about ½"
1 large red pepper seeded and diced
2 ribs celery diced
1 32 oz. box low sodium vegetable broth, (or 4 cups homemade)
2-4 cups water
1 tsp ground cumin
1/2 tsp ground coriander
1/2 tsp sea salt or to taste
½ tsp smoke paprika
1/3 tsp ground pepper
1 large avocado diced
1 Tbl cilantro minced
1/3 cup vegan sour cream (optional)

In a large pot over medium heat, saute the onion, celery, sweet potato and bell pepper in ¼ c. water or vegetable broth until they start to soften and the onion becomes translucent.

Add 3 cups of homemade black beans or 2 canned black beans to the pot plus 2 cups water and all of the vegetable broth.

Add cumin, coriander, smoked paprika, salt and pepper.

Simmer on medium until the vegetables and sweet potatoes are soft, about 30 minutes.

Transfer about half of the soup, slightly cooled, into a blender and blend until smooth. Then pour back into the pot and stir well. Or use an blender to cream part of the soup in the pot.

Serve topped with diced avocado and a sprinkling of minced cilantro. If you choose, add a dollop of vegan sour cream.

Authors Note

Black Beans should definitely be a part of your diet, you can eat these along with your tacos on Taco Tuesday, scoop with some tortilla chips, pour over nachos or eat the soup solo topped with diced avocados, sliced green onions, chopped tomatoes, fresh lime and/or hot sauce. Nutritional benefits are:

Black Beans

- High in fiber which helps with constipation and bloating
- Helps lower cholesterol levels
- Magnesium which is great for your bones
- Potassium which is great for blood pressure
- Protein

Avocados, are just plain and simply…lit, they are packed with all the good stuff your body needs. People used to say an apple a day but it should be an avocado a day…

- Vitamin K, C, B5, B6, E
- Higher in potassium than a banana
- Great fatty acid
- Fiber
- Lower cholesterol
- Heart health

Photo Credit & Food: Shanta Lamarr

Author Note:

I guess by now you have seen a little pattern…beans and legumes, I was NOT a huge fan of them before I started reducing meat and dairy from my diet. The only beans I enjoyed were BBQ baked beans and when my grandmother would make succotash, which is a tomato-based soup with lima beans, corn, okra and chunks of stewed tomatoes. Once I starting reducing meat and dairy from my diet, I started losing a lot of weight and one thing about being African American is we CANNOT lose weight too fast because people assume the worst.

In addition, I wanted to still look healthy and have a little bit of curve. One food that kept showing up repeatedly in my research was to eat more beans and legumes. I had to figure out how to incorporate these more into my diet. I had to go back to my roots and started creating all kinds of soups using a variety of beans and legumes.

You will learn as you start reducing meat and dairy while replacing them with healthier alternatives or even foods, your palate will change to grow accustomed to these foods. After I started eating more beans and legumes, I started exploring with other ways to prepare them outside of soups. Wait, I will save those recipes for the Series II: Plant based sides.

The reality is that most people cannot cut meat and dairy out of their diet cold turkey (no pun intended) I didn't! I had to be realistic with myself and I want to do the same with you. If you start with incorporating more plant-based options in your diet little by little you are making a difference in your health. Do not feel as if you do not become a hard-core vegan overnight that you are not making a difference, becoming totally plant-based takes more than the action but also knowledgeable about foods. Allow this time to be a journey, enjoy the journey, learn about foods, your body and most of all have fun trying out new recipes. Historically, beans are a huge part of African Americans die. Beans and legumes are low in fat but high in protein, fiber, they reduce the risk of cancer, balance blood sugar, heart healthy and very cost effective. Here is a list of some beans and legumes to incorporate in your diet:

Beans and Legumes

- Lentils
- Chickpeas
- White Beans
- Roman Beans
- Split Peas
- Pinto Beans
- Kidney Beans
- Black Beans
- Navy Beans
- Lima Beans

Vegetable Broth

Inspired by Rufus Estes, Good Things to Eat, The First Cookbook by an African American Chef

Serving- 6 cups of broth

1 tablespoon olive oil
1 large onion (you can leave the skin on which adds color)
5 stalks celery chopped into large chunks
3 large carrots (you don't need to peel them)
1/3 head broccoli or other vegetable broken into chunks
4 cloves garlic with skin on
3 cups greens rough chopped
2 tomatoes chopped into large chunks
1/2 bunch parsley
4 oz. mushrooms cut in half
2 bay leaves
1 tsp whole black peppercorns
½ tsp sea salt (optional)
10 cups water

Chop the vegetables into large chunks.

In a large pot over medium high heat, sauté the onions in olive oil until fragrant (about 2 minutes). Add garlic and sea salt and cook another 30 seconds.

Add the rest of the ingredients into the pot along with the water and bring to a boil. Gently stir to combine.

Simmer covered on low heat for about 1 hour. The longer you simmer it, the more concentrated it will be.

Strain the broth through a large colander to remove the larger pieces and then through a fine-mesh strainer to remove the rest.

I use vegetable broth A LOT, for my soup, stews, gravy, beans, legumes, vegetables, rice, etc., it gives your food really great flavor. Using vegetable broth combined with the right spices and health oils gives your food the flavor you need that most people think they have to use meat to get. Keep in an air-tight container(s) or for smaller quantities, freeze in ice cube trays. Allow to cool and then refrigerate.

Photo Credit & Food: Shanta Lamarr

Author Notes:

Cooking isn't anything new to me, anyone that knows me, knows that I have always loved to eat AND cook. My grandmother Mayrose, as I previously stated, was the first chef in my life, she use to tell me, "You don't cook, you don't eat" so watching her in the kitchen and just being plain greedy, I begin cooking very early in life. I had never thought about writing my own cookbook, the idea was presented to me over and over during my food journey because I was sharing the foods I was preparing through my social media. While doing research I came across, Rufus Estes, the first African American chef to publish a cookbook.

Rufus Estes, Born a slave in 1857, Rufus Estes worked his way up from a Pullman Private Car attendant to a job preparing meals for the top brass at one of the country's largest steel corporations. Rufus published this cookbook as a way to guide other slaves who were cooks, to be able to cook great meals for their masters, he was sharing the knowledge he gained on his journey to enlighten and make things easier for his people. While reading the cookbook, I was so inspired that I named my book in honor of him.

I feel that although our journeys are very different, what we are trying to achieve is the same which is to enlighten and by providing knowledge to our people. I realized that Rufus was a very talented chef and although during slavery people of color did not have access to a lot of the same foods that other chefs would have. Therefore, creative minds proved that the ability to cook delicious, hearty meals was there. Because of our ancestors sacrifice we have the ability to cook, eat and feed our families healthy, delicious options. This book is in honor of all the African American cooks, whether professional or ones that cooked for their families. Thank you to all our ancestors for the sacrifice so that we can have committed to feeding the soul and the physical body.

Better Things to Eat...

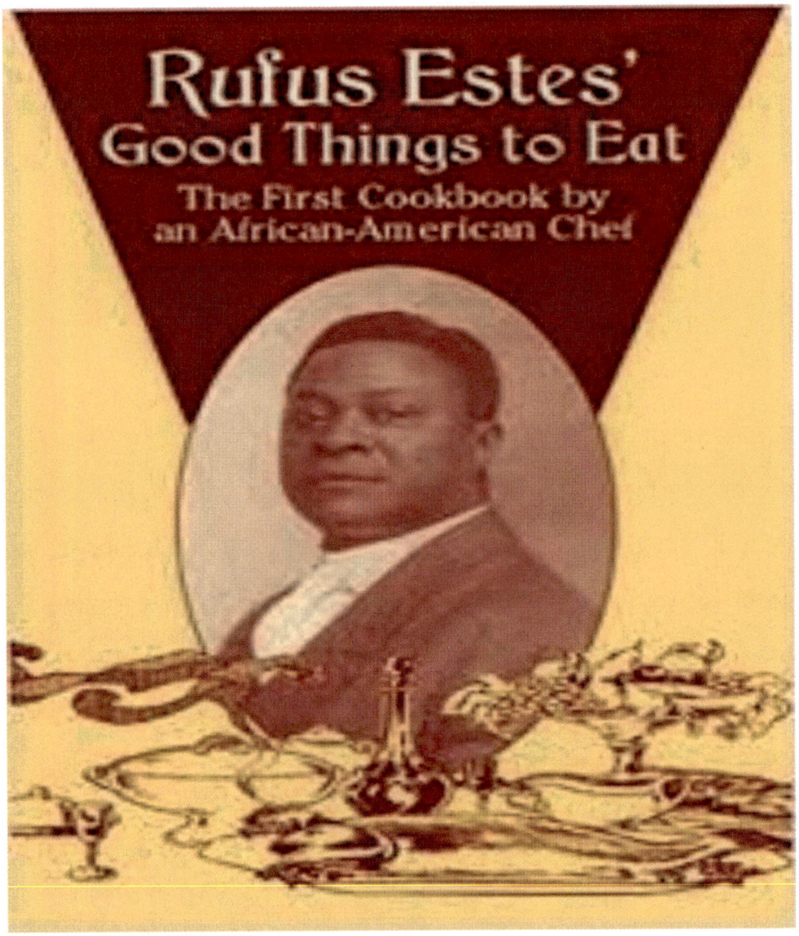
Rufus Estes'
Good Things to Eat
The First Cookbook by
an African-American Chef

Caribbean Black-Eyed Peas Stew
Serves 8

1 1/2 cups black eyed peas. Soak the dry peas in water overnight or for eight hours and then cook in a pressure cooker or in a pot, with enough water to cover, for an hour or until the peas are really tender but not falling apart.
1 tbsp olive oil
1 tbsp garlic, minced
1 large onion, diced
2 medium potatoes, diced
2 small carrots, diced
1 sweet potato, diced
1 bell pepper, any color is fine, diced
1/2 scotch bonnet pepper, use habanero as a substitute-- use less because it's spicier
1 tsp ground ginger
1 tsp ground allspice
1 tsp ground cardamom
2 tsp dry thyme
1 tsp ground black mustard seeds
Salt to taste
1 cup coriander leaves, cilantro, minced

Heat the oil and add the onions and garlic. Sauté until brown spots appear on the onions.

Add t powdered spices-- the ginger, allspice, cardamom and mustard and stir to mix well.

Add carrots, sweet potatoes, bell peppers and potatoes and stir to mix.

Add black-eyed peas, scotch bonnet pepper, thyme, coriander leaves, and enough water to make a stew. Stir well to mix.

Bring the stew to a boil, cover, lower heat, and simmer 20 minutes or until all the flavors have melded together.

Stir in the cilantro, add salt to taste. Serve hot with some rice or bread.

Photo Credit & Food: Shanta Lamarr

Vegan Jackfruit Stew

Serves 4

3 tsp olive oil divided (extra virgin)
1 bay leaf
5 cloves garlic (minced)
1 small white onion (finely chopped)
18 oz of canned drained young jackfruit
32 oz Vegetable Broth
5 med red potatoes (chopped)
4 large carrots (diced)
4 large celery stalks (diced)
2 tbsp of vegan Worcestershire sauce
1 cup of dry red wine (can sub for additional broth)
1 tbsp fresh rosemary
1 tsp dried thyme
1 tsp sea salt
1 tsp black pepper
2 tbsp corn starch

Pre- heat the oven to 400 degrees F, heat 1 tsp olive oil in large fry pan. Add bay leaf and onion, sauté for 5 minutes

Add garlic and cook for a minute, then add the jackfruit and cook on medium for another minute.

Add red wine, Worcestershire sauce, thyme, rosemary, salt and pepper, stir and bring to a gentle simmer

In a measuring cup/ bowl, whisk together the broth and cornstarch until fully combined and then mix into the skillet with the jackfruit. Bring to a simmer and let cook for 5 minutes, stirring often.

Pour the jackfruit mixture over top of the carrots and potatoes and bake for 40 minutes or until the veggies are fork tender and ready to eat. Let cool slightly and enjoy!

The flavors in this dish were amazing, my grandmother used to make the BEST beef stews, I used to get in trouble all the time for being in her pots eating all the potatoes and carrots. I remember the gravy being so good, so this dish really brought back some great memories for me, this is great paired with cabbage, corn bread or soft rolls.

Jackfruit is an exotic fruit grown in tropical regions of the world, many vegans and vegetarians use it as a meat alternative because of its texture which is similar to shredded meat. Nutritional benefits of Jackfruit include:

- Protein
- Fiber
- Helps with blood sugar management
- High amounts of Vitamin C
- Heart Health

Photo Credit & Food: Shanta Lamarr

Creamy Vegan Broccoli Cauliflower Soup

Servings- 4

1 head cauliflower
4 stalks of celery
½ red pepper (seeded, finely chopped)
1 medium onion chopped
1 regular size potato peeled and cut into cubes
2 large carrots peeled and chopped
1 bulb garlic
1/2 cup chickpeas no salt added (Eden Brand)
4 cups low sodium vegetable broth Trader Joe's brand, (or 4 cups homemade)
1/4-1/2 cup nutritional yeast
1 tsp sea salt or to taste
1/2 tsp ground pepper
1 large lemon juiced
1/3 tsp cayenne pepper or Tabasco

Preheat the oven to 425°F. Chop cauliflower into florets. Arrange on a baking sheet along with the carrots, celery, red pepper, potatoes, and season with salt and pepper.

Cut the top off the garlic bulb so that some of the cloves are slightly exposed. Season with salt and pepper. Wrap bulb in tin foil and place on sheet with vegetables.

Roast for 20–25 minutes until the cauliflower is starting to brown and the vegetables are soft.

Allow the veggies to cool then add them to a high powered blender. Squeeze the garlic out of it's skin and add it to the blender, as well.

Add the chickpeas and nutritional yeast to the blender

Pour in vegetable stock, lemon juice, cayenne pepper and additional salt and pepper, and blend on high until smooth and creamy. Taste and adjust seasonings as desired.

Pour into a large pot and simmer to heat through, adding more water as necessary to thin.

Authors Note:

Grandmother Mayrose would make a casserole with broccoli, cauliflower, cream of mushroom and cheese, I loved it! I never experimented with cauliflower outside of that dish but as I started to expand my palate, I learned a lot of different ways to incorporate it in my diet. Benefits of Cauliflower are:

- high in fiber
- minerals to boost your body's immune function
- components to fight off cancer
- lowers bad cholesterol
- improves digestion
- detoxifies
- anti-inflammatory
- aids in weight loss
- aids in eye and brain health

Nutritional Yeast, is a very nutritious vegan food product with a lot of health benefits, like adding extra protein, vitamins, minerals and antioxidant to meals. One of the main benefits is high in B-12, which is found naturally in shellfish and red meat, B-12 also aids in weight loss by helping the body to break down fats and protein into energy.

Photo Credit & Food: Shanta Lamarr

Smoky Vegan Quinoa Chili

Servings- 4

1 tbsp extra virgin olive oil
1 small sweet onion, diced
4 cloves garlic, minced
1 1/2 tsp smoked paprika
1 1/2 tsp cumin
1/2 tsp cayenne pepper
2 tbsp chili powder
1/2 tsp sugar
2 C cooked quinoa
1 C vegetable broth
1 15oz can spicy red pepper diced tomatoes
1 28oz can petite diced tomatoes
1 15oz can black beans
1 15oz can light red kidney beans
1 4.5 oz can dice green chilies
1 7oz can tomato paste
2 8oz cans tomato sauce

Heat the olive oil in a large soup pot such as a dutch oven. Add the onion and sauté until tender. Add the garlic and sauté 1 more minute. Add the smoked paprika, cumin, cayenne pepper and chili pepper to the onion/garlic mixture and mix well. Cook for 2-3 minutes in order to bring out the flavors of the spices.

Add the remaining ingredients and mix well. Cover and simmer for 30 minutes.

Photo Credit & Food: Shanta Lamarr

Cabbage Soup

Serves 5

1 tbsp extra virgin olive oil (optional)
2 cloves of garlic, chopped
1 celery strip, chopped
1/2 onion, chopped
1 carrot, chopped
1/2 red bell pepper, chopped
1-pound cabbage (450 g), chopped
1 tbsp Italian seasoning (optional)
1/2 tsp salt
1/4 tsp ground black pepper
2 bay leaves
4 cups vegetable stock or water (1 liter)
1 14-ounce can of crushed tomatoes (400 g)

Heat the oil in a large pot and add the garlic, celery and onion. Cook over medium-high heat for about 5 minutes or until golden brown. If you don't eat oil, just use some water or vegetable stock instead.

Add all the remaining ingredients and bring to a boil. Then simmer for 30 minutes.

Remove the bay leaves and serve immediately (I added some chopped, fresh parsley on top) or keep leftovers in an airtight container in the fridge for 4-5 days.

Photo Credit & Food: Shanta Lamarr

Potato Corn Chowder

Serves 4

1/4 cup water or vegetable broth
1 cup onion chopped finely
1 cup red bell pepper seeded and chopped (reserving 1/4 cup for garnish)
2 ribs celery chopped
2 cloves garlic minced
½ tsp red pepper flakes optional
1 medium potato peeled and diced
2 cups corn from 3 ears or frozen
2 Tbl nutritional yeast (optional)
½ tsp sea salt
2 cups low sodium vegetable broth (or 2 cups homemade)
1 cup unsweetened non-dairy milk
1 Tbls (shallot, dill weed, parsley and chives) Not required, but tasty.
juice of ½ lemon
sea salt and pepper to taste
Garnish
fresh cilantro
green onion chopped
red pepper chopped

In a large pot over medium heat, add ¼ cup water or vegetable broth and sauté onion, garlic, red pepper and celery for 10 minutes or until soft.

Add diced potato, vegetable broth, and non-dairy milk and mix well.

Add spices, nutritional yeast, and lemon and stir to combine. Bring to a boil. Once at a boil, reduce to simmer, cover the pan with a lid and simmer gently for 15-20 minutes, or until potatoes are tender.

Once the potatoes are tender, add corn kernels and stir to combine. Let cook for a further 5-10 minutes or until corn is tender to your liking.

Transfer about a third of the soup to a blender, and blend until smooth. Or use an immersion blender to cream part of the soup in the pot.

Pour back into the pot and stir well. Add salt and pepper to taste.

Top each serving with chopped green onion, cilantro and extra bits of corn and red pepper.

Photo Credit & Food: Shanta Lamarr

Authors Notes:

All the soups that I have provided were all customized to my pallete. During your food journey, you want to be realistic with yourself. The reality is you have to enjoy the foods that you consume. Isn't this why it is so hard to let go of meat and dairy? Because it tastes so good, use that same concept with your new lifestyle. I always say, 'as long as it tastes good, it should not matter if there is no meat or dairy, your ultimate goal is to create healthy food taste flavorful without making it unhealthy.'

It is not hard to do; it just takes a commitment to wanting to while adjusting to a new way of eating. The way I have chosen to set the series of books is that we all are in the transitional stage. All of these recipes in this first series are recipes you can eat on its own or along with a traditional meal.

As each series is introduced, you will see more and more option to remove and replace meat and dairy from your diet until eventually all or most of your meals are totally plan-based. If you are intentional with your meals and your new way of eating, you will understand that you eat to live not live to eat, your body needs these nutrients to operate properly.

On the next page, I have provided a suggested shopping list of items I feels are a must have in your home, to be able to create nutritious healthy meals. If these items are already available it makes it a lot easier to choose these over unhealthy foods. Just take it one meal at a time, I have provided a 14-day meal planner as well, as a way for you to intentional add, where you can, other healthy meal options. I hope that you enjoy the recipes and thank you for supporting me!

BETTER THINGS TO EAT
Suggested Shopping List

Vegetables
- Yellow and Red onions-A
- Sweet Potatoes
- Whole, Diced and Crushed Tomatoes
- Bell Peppers (any color(s)-A
- Celery
- Broccoli
- Kale-A
- Mushrooms-A
- Red and White Potatoes
- Cauliflower
- Corn
- Okra-A
- Green Beans
- Turnip
- Green Chili
- Scotch Bonnet or Habanero
- Shallots

Beans
- Red, brown or green lentils
- Black Beans
- Chickpeas-A
- Lima Beans
- Kidney Beans
- Chili Beans
- Black Eyed Peas

Spices and Seasoning
- Minced Garlic
- Curry Powder
- Coriander
- Cinnamon
- Turmeric
- Cardamom
- Cilantro
- Paprika
- Cumin
- Parsley
- Thyme-A
- Tarragon-A
- Celery Seed
- Minced Ginger
- Garam Masala
- Red Pepper flakes
- Chives
- Chili Powder
- Agave-A
- Allspice
- Black Mustard Seeds
- Pure Sea Salt-A
- Bay Leaves-A
- Rosemary

Misc.
- Oil (avocado, grapeseed, hempseed) A
- Coconut Milk
- Veggie Broth
- Non diary milk
- Avocado-A
- Sour cream
- Jack Fruit
- Red Wine
- Cornstarch
- Flour
- Nutritional Yeast
- Lemon Juice
- Cayenne Pepper or Tabasco sauce
- Tomato Paste
- Quinoa-A
- Tomato Sauce

Better Things to Eat

14 Day Plant Based Meal Planner

WEEK-1 PLANT BASED MEAL PLAN

	MONDAY	TUESDAY	WEDNESDAY	THURSDAY	FRIDAY	SATURDAY	SUNDAY
BREAKFAST	Strawberry Smoothie Bowl	Bagel With Coconut Cream	Plant Based Pancakes	Raspberries Coconut Pudding	Waffles With Flaxseed	Overnight Oat Pudding	Muesli Breakfast Bowl
LUNCH	Avocado Salad Bowl	Grilled Veggies	Cauliflower Falafel	Chickpeas & Rice Soup	Quinoa, Chick Peas & Kale Bowl	Hummus with Veggies & Rice Bowl	Buddha Bowl With Baked Potatoes
DINNER	Mulligatawny Soup	Roasted Tomato Pepper Bisque	Black Bean Soup	Caribbean Black Eyed Peas Stew	Vegan Irish Stew	Creamy Vegan Broccoli cauliflower soup	Smoky Vegan Quinoa Chili
SNACK	Red Velvet Smoothie	Blackberries Smoothie In Cream	Purple Blueberry Smoothie	Chocolate Truffle	Chocolate Truffle	Cocoa & Coconut Mini Waffles	Blueberry Coconut Ice Cream

WEEK-2 PLANT BASED MEAL PLAN

	MONDAY	TUESDAY	WEDNESDAY	THURSDAY	FRIDAY	SATURDAY	SUNDAY
BREAKFAST	Raspberries Coconut Pudding	Waffles With Flaxseed	Overnight Oat Pudding	Muesli Breakfast Bowl	Strawberry Smoothie Bowl	Bagel With Coconut Cream	Plant Based Pancakes
LUNCH	Quinoa, Chick Peas & Kale Bowl	Hummus with Veggies & Rice Bowl	Buddha Bowl With Baked Potatoes	Avocado Salad Bowl	Grilled Veggies	Cauliflower Falafel	Chickpeas & Rice Soup
DINNER	Vegan Corn Chowder	Southern Succotash Stew	Lentil Soup With Kale	Mulligatawny Soup	Roasted Tomato Pepper Bisque	Black Bean Soup	Caribbean Black Eyed Peas Stew
SNACK	Purple Blueberry Smoothie	Chocolate Truffle	Chocolate Truffle	Cocoa & Coconut Mini Waffles	Red Velvet Smoothie	Blackberries Smoothie In Cream	Blueberry Coconut Ice Cream

Strawberry Smoothie Bowl

Prep Time   10 Min

Total time   10 Min

Servings   1 Breakfast

1 cup coconut water
1/3 cup unsweetened shredded coconut
2 tbsps. chia seeds
1 cup chopped strawberries, plus more for garnish

- Blend all ingredients in food processor and blend on high speed.
- Pour pudding in bowl and let stand for 2 hours in fridge.
- Top pudding with strawberries and coconut flakes.
- Serve and enjoy!

BAGEL WITH COCONUT CREAM

Prep Time	10 Min
Cooking time	30 Min
Total time	40 Min
Servings	4
Breakfast	

1/2 cup ground flax seed
1/2 cup tahini
1/4 cup psyllium husks
1/2 cup water
1 tsp. baking powder
pinch of salt
sesame seeds for garnish
2 oz. coconut cream

- Preheat oven to 375F.
- To a mixing bowl, add psyllium husk, ground flax seeds, baking powder, and salt, and mix until thoroughly combined.
- Add the water to the tahini, and whisk until combined.
- Stir the dry ingredients into the wet, and then knead to form the dough.
- Lay on your baking tray and cut a small circle from the middle of each round.
- Bake for around 30 minutes, until golden brown.
- To enjoy, cut in half and spread coconut cream.

PLANT BASED PANCAKES

Prep Time   10 Min

Cooking time   10 Min

Total time   20 Min

Servings   1

Breakfast

2 tbsps. almond butter

1/4 cup almond milk
1 tbsp. ground flax
1 tbsp. coconut flour
1 tbsp. dates syrup

- Heat your frying pan on low medium heat and grease with coconut oil.
- In a small dish, mix all ingredients.
- Let this sit for 3-5 minutes, so the flax and coconut flour can absorb the liquid.
- Spoon the batter onto your skillet and spread gently into pancakes.
- Cook for about 4-5 minutes, until the pancake flips easily.
- When golden on the underside, flip and cook for another 2-3 minutes until done.
- Top with berries and enjoy!

RASPBERRY COCONUT PUDDING

Prep Time	15 Min
Cooking time	15 Min
Total time	30 Min
Servings	2

Breakfast

3 tbsps. chia seeds
1 cup almond milk
1 tsp. vanilla extract
½ cup coconut cream

STRAWBERRY JAM

1 cup raspberries, frozen

1 tsp. coconut sugar

TOPPINGS

1 tsp. raspberries jam
Berries, fresh or frozen

- Mix chia seeds, almond milk and vanilla in a jar or container. Stir and refrigerate overnight.
- In the morning, remove from fridge.
- In a pan, place frozen strawberries and coconut sugar and cook on low for about 15 minutes. Then, with an immersion blender blend the jam smooth and cook for another 2 minutes.
- For serving, jam in jar, add a layer of chia pudding and top with a layer of coconut milk.
- Top with some jam and berries (fresh or frozen).
- Serve and enjoy

MORNING COFFEE

Prep Time	5 Min
Total time	5 Min
Servings	1

Breakfast

1 cup organic coffee
1 tbsp. coconut oil
1/4 cup almond milk
1 tsp. maple syrup

- Blend freshly brewed coffee with the rest of ingredients in a blender.
- Coconut oil blends better with hot coffee.

WAFFLES WITH FLAXSEED

Prep Time	5 Min
Cooking time	5 Min
Total time	10 Min
Servings	2

Breakfast

1 tbsp. flaxseed meal
2 tbsps. warm water
¼ cup coconut milk
2 tbsps. coconut flour
¼ cup chopped mint
pinch of salt
2 oz. blueberries

- Preheat waffle maker according to manufacturer instruction and grease with cooking spray.
- Mix together flaxseed meal and warm water and wake flax egg.
- After 5 minutes' mix together flax egg with other ingredients in bowl.
- Pour batter into the center of the waffle iron.
- Close the waffle maker and let cook for 3-5 minutes
- Once cooked remove the waffles from waffle maker.
- Sprinkle berries on top and enjoy!

OVERNIGHT OAT PUDDING

Prep Time 5 Min

Cooking time 10 Min

Total time 15 Min

Servings 4

Breakfast

1 banana
3/4 cup almond milk
2 tbsps. dates syrup
Pinch sea salt
1 cup rolled oats
1 1/2 tbsps. chia seeds

1 cup strawberries sliced

- Blend the banana, almond milk, dates syrup, and sea salt in a blender till smooth.
- Place the oats and chia seeds in an airtight container. Pour the liquid
- mixture over the oats and chia seeds and mix well.
- Cover and refrigerate overnight.
- In the morning, mix again and add some milk.
- Top with fresh strawberries slice and enjoy.

MUESLI BREAKFAST BOWL

Prep Time 10 Min

Cooking time 20 Min

Total time 30 Min

Servings 2

Breakfast

1 cup muesli
2/3 cup coconut milk
1/4 cup blueberries
1 apple sliced with skin
1 oz. roasted pumpkin seeds

- Add 1 cup muesli to a medium sized bowl with milk and soak for about 20 minutes or overnight.
- Once tender and soft
- Serve soaked muesli with an apple slice, blueberries, pumpkin seeds.
- Serve and enjoy!

AVOCADO SALAD BOWL

Prep Time   10 Min

Total time   10 Min

Servings   6

Lunch

1 small avocado, mashed
3 tbsps. green onion, finely chopped
2 tbsps. lime juice
1/8 tsp. sea salt
1/8 tsp. black pepper
2 tomatoes, chopped
2 tbsps. chopped parsley

- Mix together avocado, green onion, lime juice, salt, parsley and black pepper in small mixing bowl.
- Mix well.

GRILLED VEGGIES

Prep Time 5 Min
Cooking Time 25 Min
Total Time 30 Min
Serves 2
Lunch

8 oz. small cauliflower florets

1 tbsp. olive oil

Salt

Pepper

8 oz. green peas

2 tbsp. lemon juice

Hot sauce, for serving

- Mix oil salt, pepper in pan and brush it over vegetables
- Set vegetables in greased baking
- Sprinkle lemon juice over roasted ☐ 2 summer squash, slice veggies.
- Serve with hot sauce and enjoy.

CAULIFLOWER FALAFEL

Prep Time	05 Min
Cooking Time	15 min
Total Time	20 Min
Servings	2
	Lunch

2 cups cauliflower rice
1 cauliflower head
1 small red onion minced
4 garlic cloves minced
1/2 cup cilantro leaves minced
1/4 cup coconut flour
1 chia egg
1 tsp cumin powder
1/2 tsp chili powder
1 tbsp. olive oil

- Blend herbs and spices, onions, garlic, chili, cumin seeds, cilantro and garlic to a food processor.
- Mince well and transfer to a bowl.
- In a large bowl add cauliflower rice, minced herbs, and dry ingredients, almond flour and coconut flour, salt and pepper to taste. Mix well.
- Add chia egg (mix 1 tbsp. of chia powder with 3tbs of water. Set aside till an egg-like mixture is formed) and mix well.
- Take a small ball sized dough or mixture on greased palm and form a ball. Flatten a little to make small, round falafels. Place on a greased baking sheet.
- Preheat the oven to 350F. Bake the falafels for 15-20 minutes till brown.
- Serve with corn flour tortilla and garlic mayo.
- Enjoy!

QUINOA, CHICK PEAS & KALE BOWL

Prep Time   10 Min
Cooking Time   40 Min

Total Time   10 Min

Servings   4

Lunch

1 bunch kale
1 can chickpeas
1 cup mung beans
1 cup quinoa
1 sweet potato
1 tsp cumin seed powder
salt and pepper to taste
1 lime juice
1 tsp chilli powder
salt and pepper to taste
1 tbsp. lemon juice
2 tbsps. olive oil
1 tsp. black sesame seeds

- Heat oil in pan over medium heat, add chickpea with some salt, pepper, cumin seeds and chilli powder and sauté for 3-4 minutes.
- Meanwhile place mung beans with 3 cups water in pan with salt and pepper and cook for 30 minutes until cooked and water in dried.
- Place quinoa with 1 cup water in pan with salt and pepper and cook for 10 minutes until cooked through.
- Sautee kale with oil in pan until wilted. season with salt, pepper and cumin seeds.
- Boil sweet potato in salted water for 20 minutes until cooked, cut into bite size.
- For serving divide cooked quinoa, mung beans, chick peas, kale and sweet potatoes in serving bowls.
- Slightly mix, drizzle lime juice and sesame seeds on top.
- Serve and enjoy!

HUMMUS WITH VEGGIES & RICE BOWL

Prep Time	10 Min
Cooking Time	30 Min
Total Time	40 Min
Servings	4

Lunch

1 can kidney beans

1 lb. mushrooms

salt and pepper to taste.

½ tsp chili powder
1 pinch cumin seeds
1 pinch turmeric powder
1 tsp, olive oil

HUMMUS

1/4 cup tahini

1/4 cup lemon juice

1 tbsp. olive oil

   1 cup chickpeas, boil
   1/4 tsp. sea salt
   1/4 tsp. cayenne pepper
   1/4 tsp. ground turmeric
   1 tbsp. parsley, chopped

CAULIFLOWER RICE

 1 tsp. garlic, minced
 1/4 cup white onion
1 medium head cauliflower, grated into rice
1 pinch sea salt
1 pinch turmeric powder

SERVING

1 avocado, chopped
½ head cauliflower, cut into florets
2 large tomatoes, sliced
1 lemon, sliced
lettuce leaves
2 oz. sprouts
1 tbsp. sesame seeds

- Heat oil in pan and add beans, spices and sauté for 2-3 minutes. Set aside.
- Heat oil in same pan and Sautee mushrooms with salt, pepper, chili powder, cumin seeds, and turmeric powder for 3-4 minutes. Set aside.
- Heat oil in same pan, add garlic, onion and sauté for 1-2 minutes. Add cauliflower rice followed by salt, pepper, lime juice and cumin seed powder and steam for 2-3 minutes until cooked.
- Pour hummus ingredients in blend and blend until smooth paste become.

- For cauliflower rice heat oil in and sauté onion and garlic, add rice and remaining ingredients and steam for 2-3 minutes.
- Steam cauliflower with some water in microwave.
- For serving, divide beans, rice, mushrooms, hummus, avocado, cauliflower, tomatoes, lemon, lettuce in serving bowl.
- Drizzle sprout and flax seeds on top.
- Serve and enjoy it!

BUDDHA BOWL WITH BAKED POTATOES

Cooking Time   25 Min

Total Time   35 Min

Servings   4

Lunch

1 cup sweet corn boil
5 potatoes, bakes and sliced
1 cucumber sliced
4-5 tomatoes, sliced
1 avocado, sliced
1 bunch lettuce leaves
Salt and pepper
3–4 tbsps. lime juice
3–4 tbsps. olive oil

- Bake potatoes in an oven for about 30-40 minutes until tender.
- Spread out lettuce leaves in a serving bowl.
- Set baked potatoes in middle then cucumber slice on one side, tomatoes, avocado and then sweet corns.
- Drizzle salt, pepper, lime and oil on top.
- Serve chill.
- Enjoy!

RED VELVET SMOOTHIE

Prep Time	10 Min
Total time	10 Min
Servings	2

Snack

1/2 cup strawberries, sliced

1 cup coconut water

1 cup ice cubes

1 pinch sea salt

- Blend strawberries with milk, and other ingredients into a blender, blend until thick and creamy.
- You can add water to decrease the consistency.
- Pour smoothie in serving jar.
- Top with strawberries slice.
- Serve cold and enjoy!

BLACKBERRIES SMOOTHIE IN CREAM

Prep Time   10 Min
Total time   10 Min
Servings   2
Snack

1/4 cup blueberries

1 cup coconut cream

¼ cup coconut milk

1 tbsp. coconut sugar
1/2 cup ice cubes

- Blend blueberries with cream, coconut milk, and ice cubes in blender until smooth and fluffy.
- Taste and adjust sweetener as desired.
- You can add more milk to decrease the consistency.
- Serve instantly or refrigerate until ready to serve.

PURPLE BLUEBERRY SMOOTHIE

Prep Time	10 Min
Total time	10 Min
Servings	2
	Snack

1/4 cup blueberries, fresh
½ cup coconut flour
1 cup coconut cream
1/2 cup ice
1 tbsp. coconut sugar

- Add all ingredients with ice in blender and blend until well combined.
- You can add more milk to decrease the consistency.
- Pour smoothie into a glass and top with berries and mint leaves.
- Serve & enjoy!

CHOCOLATE TRUFFLE

Prep Time	10 Min
Total time	10 Min
Servings	8

Snack

2 medium ripe avocados
1 tbsp. dates syrup
6 tbsps. cacao powder
1 tbsp. peanut butter

- Mash avocados in the bowl.
- Add sugar, cacao and peanut butter. Stir to combine.
- Put to the refrigerate for about 1 hours.
- Roll truffles and cover in the topping such as cacao powder.
- Put to the refrigerate for about 1 hour for better texture.
- Enjoy!

COCOA & COCONUT MINI WAFFLES

Prep Time   5 Min

Cooking Time 5 Min

Total Time   10 Min

Servings   2

Snack

1/2 cup coconut milk
1 tbsp. dates syrup
4 tbsps. almond flour
2 tbsps. cocoa powder
TOPPING
1 scoop coconut cream
1 tbsp. coconut flour

- Mix together all waffle ingredients in bowl and mix well.
- Preheat your dash mini waffle maker and grease with cooking spray.
- Make two mini chaffles with this batter.
- Once cooked remove chaffles from maker.
- Serve chaffles with coconut cream.
- Sprinkle some coconut flour on top.
- Enjoy with coffee!

BLUEBERRY COCONUT ICE CREAM

Prep Time 10 Min
Total time 10 Min

Servings 2

Snack

I

1/2 cup blueberries

1 cup coconut flour

2 tbsps. dates syrup

2 tbsps. coconut oil

- Heat the blueberries in a non- sticking pot on low to medium heat.
- Let the blueberries simmer for approx. 10-15 minutes until most of the liquid has dissolved.
- Add the blueberries, flour, oil and dates syrup to a food processor and blend until everything is
- combined fully.
- Transfer mixture in bowl.
- Chill in the freezer for about 10-15 minutes
- Take the mass out of the freezer and form small balls using your hands.
- Chill in the fridge for approx. 1 hour before serving.

AVOCADO AND CHOCOLATE MOUSSE

Prep Time 05 Min
Cooking time 05 Min
Total time 10 Min
Servings 2
Snack

3 oz. coconut milk
2 tbsps. dark cocoa powder
2 tbsps. dates syrup
1/2 cup avocado, mashed
1/2 tsp. ground cinnamon
1 pinch orange zest

- In a bowl, mix the coconut milk, cocoa powder, and dates syrup.
- Mix with an electronic mixer until all ingredients are combined.
- Add the avocado, and orange zest to the food processor. Blend until smooth.
- Transfer to a small bowl or round glass.
  Chill in the refrigerator for 10-20 minutes.

Made in the USA
Middletown, DE
30 March 2024